THIS BOOK BELONGS TO

_____

WITH LOVE FROM

_____

But the fruit the Holy Spirit produces is love, joy and peace. It is being patient, kind and good. It is being faithful and gentle and having control of oneself.

Galatians 5:22–23 (NIrV)

For all of the educators who lovingly and patiently plant seeds of knowledge in the minds of children. Especially those of us who are late bloomers. And for my rad dad, Robert Cameron, who was a public school teacher for over 30 years.

−XO Candace

For my beloved father who taught me everything about trees and flowers. He is always with me when I draw nature….even if some flowers I draw only grow in my imagination!

−CB

ZONDERKIDZ

Grow, Candace, Grow
Copyright © 2020 by Candache, Inc.
Illustrations © 2020 by Christine Battuz

Requests for information
should be addressed to:
Zonderkidz, 3900 Sparks Dr. SE,
Grand Rapids, Michigan 49546

Library of Congress Cataloging-in-Publication Data
Cameron-Bure, Candace, 1976- author. | Battuz, Christine, illustrator.
Title: Grow, Candace, grow / by Candace Cameron Bure ; illustrated by
    Christine Battuz.
Description: Grand Rapids, Michigan : Zonderkidz, [2020] | Summary: When
    Candace suggests that her class plant a flower garden, almost everyone
    eagerly agrees, but she finds it very hard to wait patiently for the
    plants to grow. |
Identifiers: LCCN 2019012749 (print) | LCCN 2019018033 (ebook) | ISBN
    9780310762751 () | ISBN 9780310762836 (hardcover)
Subjects: | CYAC: Gardening--Fiction. | Patience--Fiction. | Schools--Fiction. |
Classification: LCC PZ7.1.C328 (ebook) | LCC PZ7.1.C328 Gro 2020 (print) |
    DDC [E]--dc23
LC record available at https://lccn.loc.gov/2019012749

Editor: Barbara Herndon
Art direction and design: Cindy Davis

Printed in China

19 20 21 22 23 24 25 /DSC/ 20 19 18 17 16 15 14 13 12 11 10 9 8 7 6 5 4 3 2 1

GROW, CANDACE, GROW

WRITTEN BY CANDACE CAMERON BURE

ILLUSTRATED BY CHRISTINE BATTUZ

ZONDERkidz

Spring had finally arrived. For Candace that means three things—scrumptious picnics, swirly spring dresses, and most importantly . . .

FLOWERS! Big, bright, beautiful flowers. Candace could hardly wait for colorful blooms to appear.

By the time she got to school, she had an idea she was sure her teacher, Miss Fernweather, would like just as much as she did.

"We should plant a class garden," Candace announced to Miss Fernweather, smiling widely.

Miss Fernweather agreed it was a wonderful idea. So did the rest of Candace's class, especially her best friend, Sophie Rose. Harry, however, wasn't so sure. To grow a garden you need dirt, and Harry did NOT like to get dirty.

Candace's class got to work preparing to plant the garden.

They brought in shovels and seeds, watering cans and buckets, gardening gloves and a special watering hose.

When it was finally time to start planting,
Candace couldn't have been any more excited.
Harry couldn't wait to get it over with.

Miss Fernweather showed the class how to dig holes. "Not too deep," she said. Then she demonstrated how to place the seeds in the ground and cover them gently with dirt.

The class worked together . . . digging and seeding . . . until their soon-to-be garden was planted.

Candace's class stood back to admire their handiwork. But Candace wasn't impressed. There were no flowers. Just a big patch of dirt.

"When will the flowers bloom?" Candace asked Miss Fernweather.

"Plants need sunlight and just the right amount of water to grow," explained Miss Fernweather.

She showed the class how to check the soil. "When the ground feels dry, give the seeds a little drink," she said. Then Miss Fernweather gave her class an encouraging smile.

"But plants need time, so we must be patient. In about a week we'll see the seeds beginning to sprout. Then in four to six weeks, we will have bright, beautiful flowers."

Candace's class checked the garden every day. They watched and waited for the seeds to sprout.

Candace tried being patient. She really did.

But she didn't see any sign of sprouts.

Candace remembered what Miss Fernweather said: *When the ground feels dry, give the seeds a little drink.*

The ground did not feel dry, but Candace decided some extra water might help. *If a little water helps plants grow,* she thought, *then a little MORE should help them grow faster!*

So Candace gave them water.

The next day, she gave them more.

And the day after that, even more.

When the garden didn't sprout, Candace's class wanted to know why.

"It's been a week," said Megan.

"The garden had plenty of sunlight," said Christian.

"And we gave it just the right amount of water," added Sophie Rose.

Miss Fernweather checked the soil. Then she held up a handful of dark, drippy mud. "This is very odd," she said, looking up at her class. "Did someone give the garden extra water?"

Candace looked down at the ground. "I did," she said very, very softly.

"I thought a little extra water would make the flowers grow faster. I'm really sorry, everyone."

The class was not very happy with Candace.

"The garden is ruined and it's all my fault," wailed Candace. "I gave it too much water and now the seeds will never bloom."

Harry tried to cheer her up, but Candace couldn't be cheered.

That night, Candace tossed and turned in her bed.

She couldn't bear to think about her disappointed class, or teacher, or best friend, and especially about the garden they'd worked so hard to plant.

The garden would never be filled with big, bright, beautiful flowers now.

The next morning, Candace woke up with an idea.

She hurried to school, hopeful Miss Fernweather would like her plan.

"That's a very good idea, Candace," Miss Fernweather said softly. Candace had suggested that they try planting another garden. And she promised to only water it when the ground felt dry.

Candace worked hard getting ready for the new garden.

She went to visit a plant nursery.

She read about gardening.

She even brought in special seeds as a surprise for her class.

The gardener told her these flower seeds would attract beautiful butterflies!

When it was finally time to plant the new garden, Candace was excited, but a little nervous too.

She didn't want anything to go wrong. She and her class worked together, digging and planting, until everything was in place.

Candace even said a little prayer.

When they finished, they stood back to admire their handiwork. Even Harry was impressed.

Candace's class checked the garden every day. They watched and waited for the seeds to sprout and the plants to grow bigger.

It wasn't easy, but Candace waited patiently with her friends.

She only watered when the ground felt dry.

When time seemed to move slowly, she and Harry tried singing to the seeds.

At long last, sprouts appeared, and soon, little plants began to bloom. Small at first.

Then **bigger** . . . and **bigger**.

Until finally the flowers Candace had imagined blossomed big, bright, and beautiful. Colorful butterflies flitted and floated through the sea of blooms.

"It wasn't easy being patient," Candace admitted to Miss Fernweather. "But it was worth the wait."

Even Harry agreed.